to
all of us
dreamers
made of stardust
avatars of the divine presence
here on earth
in time/space
reality
now

Text copyright © 2014 by Valentina Atton
Illustrations copyright © 2014 by Sophia Johnson
Illustrations rendered in watercolor, gouache, pencil crayon and acrylic.
Book design by Iryna Spica
Typeset at SpicaBookDesign in Celestia

Production Editor: Melanie Chernyk
Copyeditors: Autumn Conley, Sally Jennings, Silvia McConnell
Early Childhood Education Consultants: Shirley Arthur, Anne Davis, Yvonne MacKenzie
Art Consultants: Hedi Kovacs, Diane Kremmer
Poetry Editors/Consultants: Eroca Dancer, Yvonne MacKenzie, Carol Ann Sokoloff
Proofreading by Pender Island Community

Printed and bound in Canada by Friesens, Altona, Manitoba.

To get permission and assistance with the *Owl's Dream* stage production, please contact Valentina.Atton@joyful-wonder-kids-press.com

Library and Archives Canada Cataloguing in Publication
Atton, Valentina, 1953-, author
Owl's Dream: a story told in poems for the young
and the young at heart / written by Valentina Atton; illustrated by Sophia Johnson.
Winner of the 2014 Moonbeam Children's Book Awards, Moonbeam Spirit Award for Imagination.
Includes bibliographical references and index.
Issued also as an audiobook.
ISBN: 978-0-9936750-1-0 (pbk)
I. Johnson, Sophia, 1989-, illustrator II. Title.

PS8601.T76094 2014   jC811'.6 C2014-902920-9

Owl's Dream ISBNs:
978-0-9936750-6-5 (audiobook), 978-0-9936750-5-8 (webPDF), 978-0-9936750-4-1 (ibook),
978-0-9936750-9-6 (soundtrack), 978-0-9936750-8-9 (play)

Summary:
Once, a great horned owl had a magical dream. In this dream various animals, big and small, tell their stories to a human child who understands them all. *Owl's Dream* reveals that we all speak the same language – the language of love.

Target audience:
Children of all ages, and artistic and spiritually sensitive adults/parents/grandparents/caregivers/educators interested in connecting with their inner child.

Each book includes a download code for the *Owl's Dream* MP3 Audiobook (page 83).
Narrated by Jan Rabson
Enchanted with music and nature sounds by Daryl Chonka
Recorded and produced at Old Growth Music Studio

Joyful Wonder Kids Press
www.joyful-wonder-kids-press.com

Owl's Dream

A Story Told in Poems
for the Young and the Young at Heart

By Valentina Atton
Illustrated by Sophia Johnson

JOYFUL WONDER KIDS PRESS

Praise for *Owl's Dream*

"Fun and magic for the whole family!"

The Islands Independent

"*Owl's Dream* is a joyful journey into a land of expression where our differences spark Oneness as we speak from our hearts."

Jan Albertin, Artist

"Delightful! And so much love!"

Barbara Stowe, Dancer, Former Instructor Vancouver Children's Circus 'Cirkids',
Creative Writing Teacher, Langara College

"*Owl's Dream* manages to blend serious wisdom with a palatable sense of joy and playfulness. I surrendered eagerly to being carried away by its beauty and insights to a delightful world of nature."

Elizabeth Scalice, Owner of Architectural Salvage of San Diego,
Grandmother, Environmentalist

"These simple truths transport me to a time when life was a lot simpler – a time in my childhood when I believed I could fly and all the animals did talk to me, along with the fairies and angels, of course."

Shakeira Wynde, Creatrix, Healer, Artist

"Interactive. Provocative. Theatrical. What a sheer delight to be taken to the world of a child and be surrounded by imagination, creativity, and joy!"

Ann Coombs, Life Coach, Writer

"Through her rhythmic prose, Valentina Atton brings to life the fellowship between human beings and nature's creatures, sparking and awakening the senses with her descriptive representations. As an educator of young children, I appreciate the endless possibilities for teachable moments, language development and programming designed to help connect children with nature."

Colleen Carpenter, Early Childhood Educator

"What a gorgeous, lush, vivid work of art! The illustrations are outstanding."

Renée Layberry, Freelance Editor, Writer

"*Owl's Dream* tickles all our senses and invites us back into the magical world of a child, where everything is possible. It is an honour to witness the unfolding of this beautiful creation and gift to the world."

Sharon Slaney, Herbalist, Nurse, Storyteller

A Note to Parents and Educators

In this book, various animals speak to your child. As you read, you serve as the
co-creator of your child's experience. The more you use your imagination
to step into the character of each animal, the closer you will be to its spirit.

We suggest that you do not announce the titles of the poems.
Let the child recognize the animal
based on Owl's introductions before each poem
and our colour-coded fonts for the animals.

Download and listen to the audiobook to help set the tone for your reading.

Wear animal masks, ears, or antennae to embody the characters you will become
in the child's imagination, as well as to make your reading more fun.

If you wish, replace the terms of endearment indicated by the

fancy font

with your child's name
to create an intimate connection
between child and animal.

Encourage your child to learn the poems by heart
and perform them for family and friends.
Owl's Dream can easily be staged as a play.

After working with these poems in many joyful ways,
don't be surprised if the poet in your child is revealed!
Just ask your child to tell a story
from the perspective of an animal that is not in this book
and then encourage, listen, and cheer.
You will be amazed by what you hear!

Have fun!

Owl's Dream

Hoo-hoo! Hoo-hoo-hoo!

I am Owl, a great horned owl,
hooting a story for you.

Once I had a beautiful dream –
snowcapped mountains on the horizon,
upland forests, and gently sloping foothills
descending into a wide, sunny valley.

In the valley was a small farm
with green fields scattered all around,
an old pond overgrown with lilies and reeds,
and a big maple tree, tall and shady,
next to the still water.

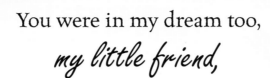

You were in my dream too,
my little friend,
sitting under the tree,
dreaming your own dream.
Many animals, big and small, came to you one by one
to share their stories.

You understood them all.
I understood them too,
and you and I understood each other,
for we all spoke the same language!

Hoo-hoo-hoo-hoo-hoo!

Hoo-hoo!

First came a butterfly with her heart song for you.

3

Butterfly's Heart Song

Hi,
little friend!
High,
so very high,
up in the sky
I fly!
I fly high!

I am a butterfly.
My name is Vi.

I fly,
and I flutter.
I flutter,
and I fly.

Now,
dropping down,
I spy flowers
on the ground.

A winking daisy,
a dewy rose,
a shy, purple violet,
a saffron primrose . . .
All full of nectar
and wonderful smells!
Some taste like licorice,
some like caramel!

4

Tickling my toes on a silky petal,
pointing my wings to the sky,
slowly unfolding the tube of my lips,
I stop.
I nestle.
I kiss
the flower!

Ardle-taba-taba-ty!!!

Which means,
in the language of Flutterby,

"My heart sings
getting ready to fly!"

But I'm not quite finished with this
flowery treat yet . . .
Leisurely I sip the nectar sweet,
sucking and slurping
every last bit.

Delightful, delectable,
yes, indeed!

How I'd love to share

this joy with you!

My little friend,

my sweetheart,

I love you!

8

Neigh!

Did you hear?
Who is asking you to play now?

Who-who?

Foal's Call

Neigh!

Hey, *buddy!* Hey!

I am a foal.
I am grey!
I am Grey Ray!
Come to the fields!
It's spring.
Let's play!

10

Jump?
Kick?
Hide-and-go-seek?
Whatever we do, let's be quick.
Be quick!

You hide, and I'll seek.
Let's play!
Hide in the grass!
Hide in the hay!
Hey-hey!

11

Now where did you go?

Shhh . . .

I hear your breath.
You must be close . . .

I part the straw
with my huge, warm nose.

I bet you've never seen
my nose so close!

Go on. Touch it.

You whisper, "Wow!"

I whisper back,
"I see you now."

12

Hoo-hoo! Hoo-hoo-hoo!

A long spring day is done.
Night comes with bright moon and stars.
Everybody is sleeping
except Milky Way and her new baby.

"Mooooo!"

The baby calf
wants to share with you
the magic and the beauty
of his very first night.

Newborn Star, the Calf's Story

Mooooo . . . Moon!
Mooooo . . . Mom!

I learned to talk the night I was born,
cooing and mooing the whole night through.
Mooooo!

Mom licked me gently
washing me off,
anointing me with her spittle.
Her tongue was so soft.

"There, sweet babe,"
my beautiful mother said.
"All nice and clean,
though still a little wet!
The sun will dry you off,
my darling pet.

The sky will welcome the sun very soon
and say goodbye to the man in the moon.

Mooooo . . .
Goo-goo-loo . . .
Precious you . . .
Mooooooo . . ."
Mom leaned down to kiss my nose.

"Oh," she said,
"I see a star upon your head!
I will name you Star, babe.

16

A shining Star
from now on you are,
and I am your Milky Way,
your galaxy!

Here is your first breakfast, Star,
and your first sunrise!
If the sun shines too brightly,
just close your eyes.

Nice warm milk for you . . .

Mooooo . . .
Goo-goo-loo . . .
Precious you . . .
Mooooooo . . .

Look, Star, look!
Look who is there.
Someone else who likes milk!
There is plenty to share."

I open my eyes and see you,

little one,
and your beautiful mother,
with a bright birthday bundle
of colourful blooms.

My mom sniffs with pleasure
at this flowery bunch,
moos a long "Thank you!"
and gulps it down:
munch . . .
munch . . .
munch . . .

17

I look at your forehead,
little avatar,

my milk sibling,

to find *your* star.

I can't see it,
but I know it's there.
Be
aware.

18

I am Star.
You are a star too.

We share the Milky Way,
our Galaxy of Light,
Sun, Moon, Star, and You.

Mooooooo!

19

Hoo-hoo! Hoo-hoo-hoo!

The sun and the moon,
the stars and the flowers,
big animals and tiny living things,
and you,
my little friend...

What a beautiful world!

20

Hoo-hoo-hoo-hoo-hoo!

Here on a green leaf,
who is this small creature?

Tree Frog's Jazzy Daydream

Cr-r-o-o-o-o-ak! Cr-r-o-o-o-o-ak!

I am Eeka, a frog.
I'm a tree frog, a free frog,
a real hide-and-go-seeker,
with my squeaky, creaky song.

I don't belong
to the pond frogs' team.
They are quite brown,
but I am all green.

Green like the leaves
that spring from the trees;
green like Granny Smith apples,
if you please.

By the way,
do you have a granny,
my sweet greenheart?
I wish I could meet her
and nicely entreat her
to share the flair
of her culinary art!

First,
all together,
the three of us,
could sit by the fire
and groove on jazz.

23

In our leaf-green jackets,
we'd sing along with the
saxophone,
"Oh, bright green leaves . . ."
in very high keys.

Later on,
down
our voices would go
to sing,
"Oh, soft green moss . . ."
low and slow.
You never know
how low
we could go!

Green moss, green leaves,
above and beneath.
Green world, green peace!
Puh-duh-buh-duh,
puh-duh-buh-duh,
green peace . . .

Keeping pace
with the big double-bass,
we'd make a cool jazzy trio,
oh, mamma mia!

And then your granny
would bake us a pie
with green Granny Smith
apples
that I wouldn't try.

Why?

Because she'd bake
a special froggy treat
just for me.

A small pie . . .
with a fly!

Oh, my!

Fly pie!

Hoo-hoo!

Let's go to the pond
where sunlight dances on water
with each breath of wind
and dragonflies dart overhead!

Put your hand up
slowly,
and here she is,
alighting on your fingertip.

Dragonfly's Reflections

Hi,

little human!

Hi!

I am Draga, the dragonfly.
Let's look at each other,
eye to eye.

My eyes are like two goldfish bowls,
where sunrays flicker and float
in the ever-changing reflections of the sky.

It comes as no surprise
that you are fascinated
by my eyes.

Swish . . . s-s-s-s-s-s . . .
Do you hear the swish of my wings
as I move closer?
Swish . . . s-s-s-s-s-s . . .

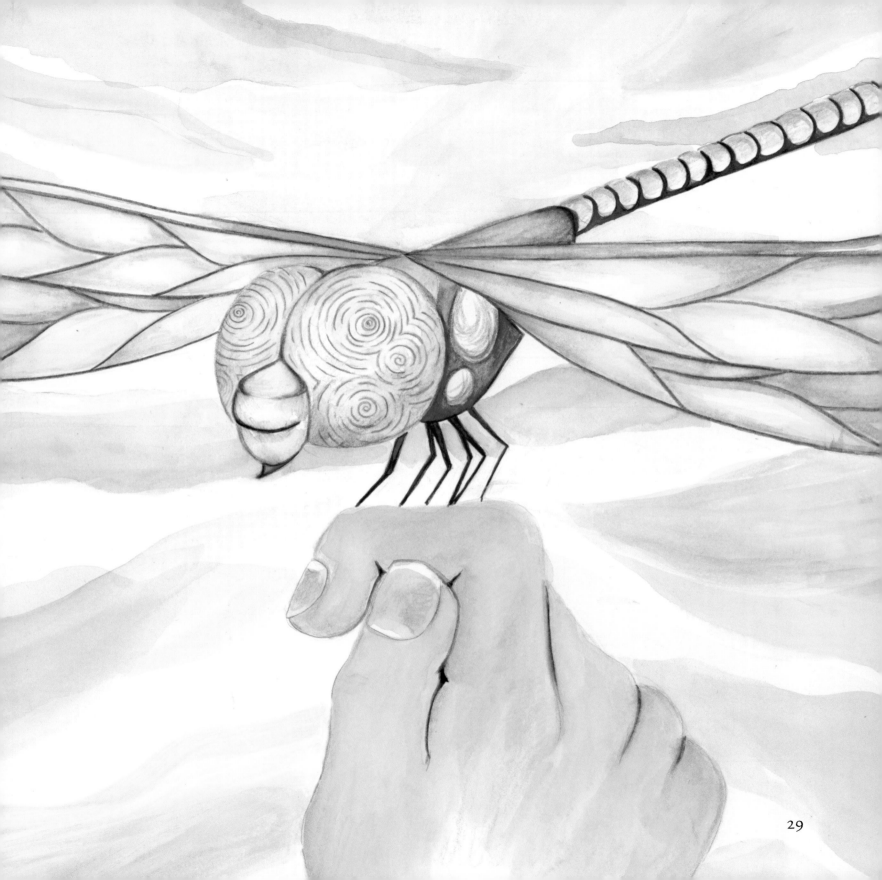

Now I see your eyes,
beautiful, curious, and wise.
You close your eyes when you go to sleep,
but now they are open and, oh, they are deep!

Deep as water wells.

If I look long enough,
I can see stars at the very bottom . . .
and whales . . . and snails . . .
and two curious dragonflies,
one in each of your luminous eyes.

Oh!
You hold the whole world in your eyes,
just like me!
What a perfect match are we!

Ever-watching,
ever-seeing
the whirling,
twirling
world
unfurls
and swirls . . .
S-s-s-s-s-s . . . swish . . .

31

Hoo-hoo...

It's so quiet here.

Flip-flop . . . Flip-flop . . .
Tiny fish jumping out,
hoping to snatch a bug or two.

Bulrushes rustling, mosquitoes buzzing . . .

Then suddenly,
a big splash!

Who is this?

Who-who?

35

Otter's Joy

I'm Otta,
an otter,
an otter's daughter.

I am water's daughter!

I flop into water
in a flash,
make a big splash,
then dash!

36

Watch me,

sweetie,

as I swim, as I glide,
rippling the water
from side to side.

Now,
in the blink of an eye,
I dive.
Goodbye, blue sky!

Hello,
underwater world,
cool and green.
Down I submerge,
like a submarine.

Holding my breath,
I soak up the scene.

37

Mom calls,
"Otta-pup, please pop up!
Time to stop
your swimming galore
and come back to shore!"

Back to shore?
What for?

I am a river otter!
I am water's daughter!

"Yes, you are,"
says mom.

"But more is true.
We otters belong to the land too.

Like long, furry needles,
we stitch together
land and water,
water and air,
until twinkling night stars
become our den's chandelier.

Goodnight, Otta.
Goodnight, land.
Goodnight, water.

Goodnight,

dear heart,

May you sleep tight
and dream your joyful dreams
throughout the night."

38

Hoo-hoo!

Thunderstorm!
Let's go to the forest
and take cover!

Hoo-hoo-hoo-hoo-hoo!

40

Wait!
Somebody is here…
a little baby fawn!
Look how precious she is.
Come over here, Spottie!

41

White-Tailed Fawn's Language

Mom taught me,
"Never speak to strangers.
Use the language
of signs."

So I do,
sweetie-pie!

If I show you my
big,
round,
brown
eyes,
it means . . .

I'm scared!
Don't move!
Stand by!

If I show you my
quivering,
twitchy,
white
tail,
it means . . .

Goodbye!

42

Hoo-hoo!

Spottie bounced away.
That was quick!
But who is this?

Who-who?

44

"Baaa-aa-aah!"

Here comes Hilda
with a story to tell.

45

Mother Sheep's Lost and Found

Baaa-aa-aah!

A few years ago, there was a long, harsh winter here.

I lost my dear ba-a-a-by
in a blizzardy storm.
I cried for many months,

until you, *my sweet,* were born!

You came to this pasture
along with your parents,
all bundled up tight
in a fine baby carriage.

I saw you and loved you –
yes, love at first sight!
Baaa-aa-aah! Baaa-aa-aah!
What joy! What delight!

Ever so kindly
and very politely,
I asked your parents
if I might pet you,
their precious new baby.

Your dad nodded his head.

Your mother said, "Yes!
You may pet our baby,
gently nuzzle our baby,
even feed our baby
if it makes you glad."

"Here's our milk bottle,"
added your dad.

Oh,
such loving trust!
At last
life is good again!

You

sweet baby,

are so very cute.
It feels like deep in my heart,
someone's playing a flute.

You are
the sweetest little lamb.
Would you call me "Mom"?

Baaa-aa-aah!

48

Hoo-hoo!

That story touched my heart deeply.

Yes,
we animals
are very much like you humans.

We live, and we love.
We laugh, and we cry.

We learn, and we wonder,
and sometimes ask, "Why?"

And each of us has
our very own nature,
like Flavio the cat —
oh, what a creature!

I'm sure he's here somewhere.

Flavio, where are you?

Cat's Feelings

Meow!
Here I am.
Here and now!

Right beside you,
little angel ,
basking in the sun on your cozy couch.

Ouch!
You put your book down on my tail!
It's rather heavy,
this fairy tale!

Could you
put your book away
and pet me, please,
restoring my purrrrrfect peace?
Please?
Please?
Please?

I like my ears to be softly touched.
I like my head to be gently scratched.
Under my chin? Sure!
Any loving touch makes me purr.

Ahhhh!
Long, slow strokes down my back?
You are really good at this!
It feels wonderful!
Purrrrrrr, purrrrrrr, pure bliss!

I'm losing track
of time and space.
My heart is melting
with love and grace.

I know you feel the same,
but please don't talk.
Just stroke.
Just stroke.
Ahhhh!

54

You and I
are here
together
now,
becoming One . . .
becoming one big, furry, purry, melting heart!
Wow!
Meow.

Hoo-hoo! Hoo-hoo-hoo!

Are you purring now?
Purrrrrrrrfect!
But don't close your eyes just yet,

sleepyhead.

I hear the distant beating
and whooshing
of many big wings,
taking flight through the sky
to come to your dreams!

57

Flamingo's Life

Flamingo!
What an exotic, ecstatic name!
Great match to our plumage of shocking pink,
with a splash of black on every beak
and under each bright wing!
This is our everyday wear
of fashionable, flashy, flamingo flair!

Bright pink bonanza
extravaganza!

58

Under the fruit trees, papaya and mango,
you'll find us dancing our own little tango.
Care for bolero? Maybe hot samba?
And how about rumba?
Playing marimba!
Flamenco!
Flamingo!

Snacking away at the algae bar,
posing for pictures in Zanzibar,
we savour each moment of our colourful, fun-filled days!
"No need to hurry," flamingo says.

The only time
you'll find us rushing,
flying, swimming, running,
speeding,
or even stampeding
is when you call us
to your dreams,

sweetheart.

We always come
to spice up your dreams,
to paint them, to make them
rumba-marimba-flamingo-tango-fandango-mango
tasty, juicy, sweet, pungent, and bright
with all the colours of the rainbow,
not just black and white!
And plenty of hot pink,
we think.
Oh, what a sight!

61

Hoo-hoo! Hoo-hoo-hoo!

Your dream is unfolding for you,
beloved...

Hoo-hoo-hoo-hoo-hoo!

Dreamland Chorus

Ribbit, ribbit!
Cr-r-o-o-o-o-ak! Cr-r-o-o-o-o-ak!
Ribbit, ribbit!
Cr-r-o-o-o-o-ak! Cr-r-o-o-o-o-ak!

Neigh!
Meow!
I see you now.

May I hug you, Miss Milky Cow?
Wow!
Free hugs, free hugs,
from a tree frog –
a free frog!
Cr-r-o-o-o-o-ak! Cr-r-o-o-o-o-ak!

Marimba!

Drum, swim, dream!
Dream, drum, swim!

And run, and jump, and swing!
and laugh, and dance, and sing!

**Whatever you do,
wherever you go,
just know:
there is love!
And there is magic!**

Zanzibar!
. . . and a back yard,
your own back yard...

Madagascar!
. . . **and a pond beside your home,
a forest, river, garden,
full of magic,
light and golden!**

Sweetheart,

sweetheart,

I love you!

Drum, dream, swim!
Swim, drum, dream!

**And fly!
On the wings of love, fly!
It feels so good!
Just try!**

What a beautiful world!
Beautiful, wonderful,
wonderful, beautiful,
beautiful, wonderful world!
Hoo-hoo!

65

Moooo!
I am over the moon!
The sun and the moon and the stars
are ours!

We are
the sun and the moon and the stars,
and Earth and Saturn and Venus and Mars!

And the moss and the leaves,
above and beneath!
"Oh, bright green leaves!"
Above and beneath,
green world, green peace!

Pure bliss,
Pure bliss . . .
Swish . . . S-s-s-s-s . . .
Bliss . . .

And
All-That-Is
is greater than imagined!

Imagine!
Imagine a wonderland,
where all your dreams come true!

Yes!
Your dreams come true!
Out of the blue!
Believe! And know!
It is true! It is so!

Wow!
Ba-a-a-ah!
Meow!

We-e-e-e-e-e-O-o-o-o-o-o-M-m-m-m-m . . .
We-e-e-e-e-e-e-Swing . . .
Wing!
Fling!
Up and away!
S-i-i-i-i-i-i-i-i-i-i-i-i-i-i-ng!

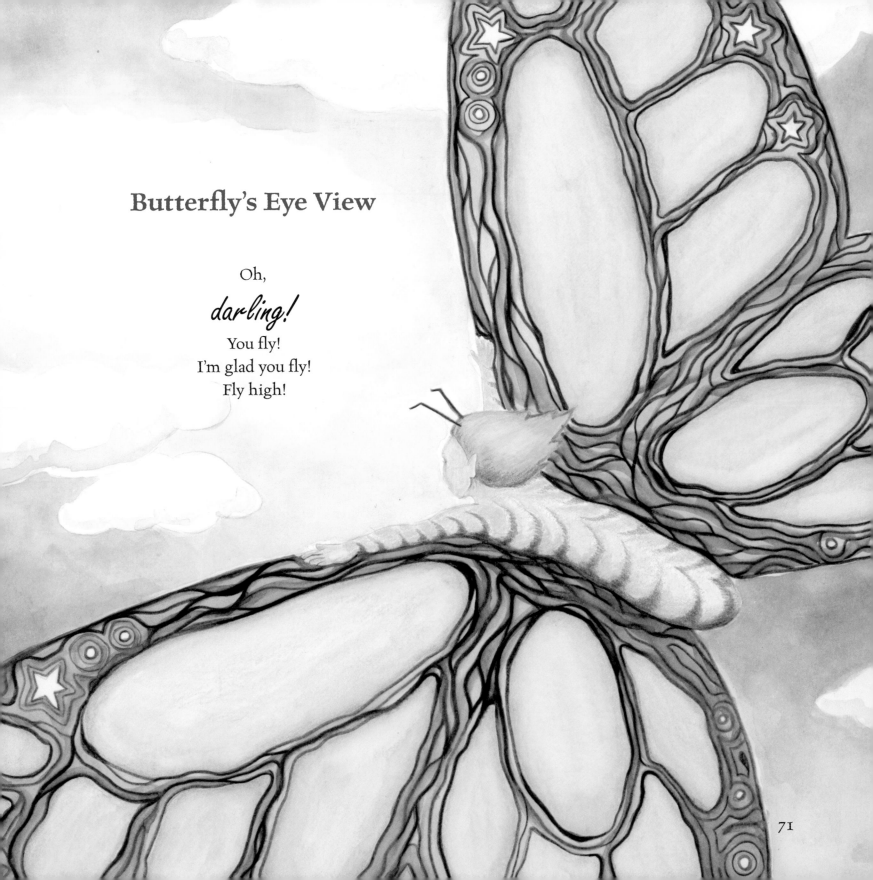

Butterfly's Eye View

Oh,

darling!
You fly!
I'm glad you fly!
Fly high!

In your dreams,
in your life,
fly!
Don't question why.
Just fly!

Like a bird,
like a bug,
like a butterfly . . .

Like me!
I fly high!

Now
let's drop down.
I spot flowers
on the ground,
all full of nectar –
a daisy, a rose,
violets and bluebells,
and a lovely primrose.

Such beautiful colours,
wonderful smells!
Some taste like honey,
some like caramel . . .

72

I am
so delighted
to share this joy with you,

my dear
little friend,
my sweetheart!

I love you!

"I love you too."

Mooo!
Ti amo
Te quiero
Baaa!
我爱你
I
Love
You
大好き
Ich liebe dich
Croak!
Hoo hoo!
Je t'aime
Я Тебя люблю
Meow!
أحبك
Neigh!

Hoo-hoo!
Hoo-hoo-hoo . . .

It's time I fly.
I'll see you in Dreamland,
at night in the sky.

For now you know
we all share one tongue
and speak the same language,
the language of love!

Hoo-hoo-hoo-hoo-hoo . . .
I love you . . .
I love you . . .
I love you . . .

Index of Poems
by colour and page number

Please note Owl introduces each poem

Acknowledgments

Thank you, Mother Earth,
for making a home for all of us –
humans, animals, and plants.

Thank you, teachers, family, friends, and pets,
for helping me become
who I really am
now.

Thank you, Higher Power, for assisting me
in the creation of *Owl's Dream*.

Thank you, wonderful Pender Islanders,
for your help, support, encouragement,
and love.

I love you too!

Thank you, from the bottom of my heart:

Ada & Ivy * Ashlyn * Jan Albertin * Jackson Allan * Helen Allison

Malcolm & Sandi Armstrong * Shirley Arthur * Trysh Ashby-Rolls * Paul Atton

Joby Baker * Clarice Bloomenthal * Ghenia Bogun * Angie Bowns * Gregg Braden

Valerie Butcher * Karin Campbell * Colleen Carpenter * Lewis Carroll

Nathalie Chambers * Jim & Anne Chernyk * Melanie Chernyk * Deryl Chonka

Deepak Chopra * Autumn Conley * Maya & Michele Cook * Ann Coombs

Nancy Coutts * Jim Cromarty * Sandor Csepregi * Dalai Lama * Eroca Dancer * Dasha

Anne Davis * Pierre Delacote * Kelly Dine * Dockside Realty * Ann Douglas

Dragonfly Child Care & Family Centre * Dr. Wayne W. Dyer * Myra Eadie * Jan Ede

Maureen Edwardson * Bruce Everett * Jude Farmer * Alison Feargrieve * Fehrgus * Megan Fisher

Lisa Fleming * Gregory Franklin * Gabriel & Olivia & Georgia * Tracey Gillespie * Karen Goldstraw

Leah Graham * Amanda Griesbach * Larry Haines * Maelle Hardy & Noah * Dave Hargreaves

Debbie Harris * Janie Harrison * Louise Hay * Ester & Jerry Hicks * Tracey Hodgins

Lydia Hol * Ernest Holms * Derek Holzapfel * Marina Horvath * Daniel Howlett * Katerina Jacob

Gail Jamieson * Sally Jennings * Sophia Johnson * Julie Johnston * Grace Jordan

Shalina Kajani * Laurie Kay * Diana & Roz Kempe * Tim Kempe * Coco Kimmitt

Kesha & Kisa * Bill Kitchen * Deirdre Knister * Charlie Knowles * Krista Konkin

Hedi Kovacs * Diane Kremmer * Kristina & Alex * Natasha Kryzhanovska

Lucie Lambert * Marlene Landa * Andrew Lane * Devrah Laval * Joan Lawrence

Renée Layberry * Michel Lemoges * Helen Lemon-Moore * Astrid Lindgren

Sadie Lucas * Jennifer Lyons * Diane MacDonald * Jacquie MacDonald-Shannon

David MacKenzie * Yvonne MacKenzie * Jolen MacLean * Lee Eschara MacNab

Jacquie Main * David Manning * Brent Marsden * Masha * Clare Mathias

Elizabeth May * Leslie McBain * Silvia McConnell * Colleen McLennan * Matthew & Sher & Phoenix

Andrea Mills * Mae Honey Moore * Tracey Moore * Myrtle Mustoe

Stephanie Newell * Thich Nhat Hanh * Julia & Gregory Nicholls * Kathryn Nimetz

Nicolas & Alexander * Linda & Stan Oglov * Aislinn O'Shaughnessy

OWL Rehabilitation Centre * Pajtas * Craig Paterson * Nicole Payer * Barb Pender

Port Washington Montessori Pre-school * Brigitte Prochaska

Ptarmigan Music and Theatre Society * Eve Pollard * Angélique Régimbal * Brad Prevedoros

Kathy Pye * Lester Quitzau * Jan Rabson * Ambé Ray * Melanie Ray * Mary Reher * Kathleen Resvick

Wilma Riley * Julie Roper * Ellie Ross * Antoine de Saint-Exupéry

Elizabeth Scalice * Adrian and Cora Schamberger * Ludmila Scherbakova

Amanda & Gabrielle Seguin * Dr. Seuss * Christine Shantz * Craig Shemilt

Catherine Sherlock * Tania Schissler * Kali Sharon Slaney * Owen Smith

Carol Ann Sokoloff * Angela Southward * Andrea Spalding * Gary Steeves

Iryna Spica * Barbara Stowe * Leslie A. Strike * Nigel Strike

Talisman Books and Gallery * The Islands Independent * Simon Thomson

Marti Tilley * Nancy Tillman * Ina Timmer * Eckhart Tolle * Marnie Toulson

Lillian Trigg * Marina Tsvetaeva * Serena Van Bakel * Murray & Sharon Vasilev

Ona Vilarmau Newell * Vishtar * Karin Von Gaza * Fred Vye * White Tara

Meave & Wren Wilde * Nia Williams * Shakeira Wynde * Candis Zell

*I am Star. You are stars too. We share the Milky Way,
our galaxy of light.* Valentina Atton

Praise for *Owl's Dream*

"In *Owl's Dream*, we learn to connect with animals, insects, plants, and their habitats through the eyes of a child – both up close and from the infinite perspective.
Readers of all ages will delight in Valentina Atton's poignant poems and Sophia Johnson's magical illustrations, which will prompt them to spend many hours
visiting and revisiting these precious pages."

Brigitte Prochaska, Film/TV Unit Publicist

"*Owl's Dream* offers inspiration for anyone looking to produce an uplifting community or school play, with many parts to suit any ability and comfort level, both on and off stage.
The poems inspire music, dance, acting, sounds, and simple, effective, affordable sets and costumes.
This book is a blueprint for bringing a community together to create a joyful bonding experience.

Owl's Dream is a wonderful resource for caregivers, parents, and teachers. It invites us to more closely observe the creatures we share our world with. Although the animals are anthropomorphized at times, they are based on careful authentic and insightful observations.
As a nanny, I read *Owl's Dream* or individual poems as a prelude to an outing together.
After reading the Dragonfly poem, I can take the children to a lake or wetland to sit quietly and listen together for the sound of dragonfly wings: swish...s-s-s-s-s.
We can look into the eyes of a dragonfly, just as the child in the poem does.

Owl's Dream is full of joy and humour and an affirmation of love for our animal and insect neighbours.
I was deeply touched to read feelings I have never articulated within the poems.
This book isn't just for kids but for all of us."

Karin Campbell, Mother, Nanny, Lover of Nature

"When one steps back for a moment from the hardness of concrete and the coldness of technology and considers the compelling draw of nature and our souls' yearning for communion, we understand – if we are the least bit willing – that we are truly interconnected with all beings; we are, in reality, one with nature, and any sense of separation from nature is an issue of perspective and illusion.

Owl's Dream by Valentina Atton has been boldly and intuitively created as a representation of the joy, beauty, and healing that comes from flowing unhindered in this connection and communion.
Coming from a quietly animistic perspective, the author has powerfully tapped into the universally recognized tendency of children to identify with non-human creatures, great and small.
Through the ancient art of wordplay, rhythm, and rhyme, *Owl's Dream* ushers readers of all ages – whether children by chronological age or children at heart –
into a sacred space where poetry and imagery are played in lyrical time with the beat of the heart and the dreamscape of the imagination."

Renée Layberry, Freelance Editor, Writer

For your complimentary *Owl's Dream* MP3 audiobook download,
please redeem the following code at our website:
22431AB
www.joyful-wonder-kids-press/shop.com
Click on the "Claim my Download" button and follow the directions.
Thank you!

Owl's Dream Audiobook

Written and directed by Valentina Atton
Narrated by Jan Rabson

Recorded and produced by Daryl Chonka
at Old Growth Music Studio,
Salt Spring Island, British Columbia, Canada
www.oldgrowthmusic.com

MUSIC

Composed by Daryl Chonka
Arranged and performed by Daryl Chonka and Craig Paterson
Recorded, sequenced and mastered by Daryl Chonka

Nature sounds by Daryl Chonka and Joby Baker

Afterword
by Valentina Atton

Dear Reader,

As you read or simply leaf through the pages of this book,
you will find joy and playfulness blended with timeless wisdom.
I believe that children intuitively know and understand
our relationship to the world around us.
Owl's Dream is inspired by my contemplation of the Universe we inhabit.
And here are some of my thoughts and words about the Universe
as it appears in *Owl's Dream*.

First of all – relax:

Nobody really knows how it all started,
although there are many theories.
Most astronomers and quantum physicists believe
the Universe began with a Big Bang,
roughly 14 billion years ago.

Bang!

In a fraction of a second, the Universe grew
from smaller than a single atom
to larger than a galaxy,
and has kept on growing at a fantastic rate.
In fact, it is still expanding today!

The Universe contains billions of galaxies,
each home to millions or billions of **stars.**
The **galaxy** we live in is called the **Milky Way**.
It is a spiral galaxy, shaped like a huge **whirlpool**,
full of **stardust**, gases, and more than 100 billion **stars**.

Our Solar System – one of many in the Milky Way –
is made up of **the Sun** and the planets, **Earth and Saturn**,
Venus and Mars, to name a few.

We live on such a beautiful planet – **Earth!**

The Sun, our closest star, provides the heat and **light**
needed to maintain **life** on our planet.
The Moon, a satellite of Earth, does not emit its own light
but only **reflects** the light of the Sun.

When you **look** at a full moon,
you **can see** the shadow of Moon's **mountains**
forming the figure of a man.
We call it "**the man in the moon**."

Here on Planet Earth, we have **air** to breathe,
water to drink, **land** to grow food,
and we **share** our planet
with many beautiful plants and **animals**!

When **animals** (mammals) give **birth,** they produce **milk,**
not only enough for their **babies** but for us humans too.
We drink milk from **cows**, just as **calves** do,
making us all **milk siblings**!

Plants breathe in
what **humans** and animals breathe out (carbon dioxide),
and humans and animals breathe in
what plants breathe out (oxygen).

We are all connected.
We are all part of this great **One**ness.

The universal **field** of energy
that connects everything in this **world**
is called the **Divine** Matrix.

You can explore the subjects of Quantum Physics, Divine **Matrix,**
Morphic Resonance, and other theories about our Universe…

or you can find all the knowledge within you!

Just **close your eyes** and stay **still** for a few moments.
Feel the **warm**th of **the sun** on your cheeks.
Listen to all the sounds around you and within **you.**
Become **aware** of your precious **breath.**
Breathe **in**… out… in again… **out**…

Sense the divine life essence in you…
in **all** other **human** beings…
in all **animals** and plants…
in the rocks, **stardust**,
planets and **galaxies**…

Written by Abigail Burlingham
Illustrated by Andy Everitt-Stewart

Published in 2006 by Autumn Publishing Ltd,
Chichester, West Sussex, UK PO20 7EQ.
© 2006 Autumn Publishing Ltd

Printed in China

Best Friends

BYEWAY
B O O K S

Willow was curled up in the chair by the fire.
Star snuggled at her feet.
I'm safe here with Willow, thought Star.

Suddenly, Willow leapt up.
"Let's go out, Star," she said. "Let's go for a ramble."
Star loved rambling with Willow.

Out into the cold went Star, Willow and her mother.
Out of the gate and up the grassy hill.

"Let's have a race," said Willow.

But Star ran too fast.
He was too far from Willow.
I'm not safe here, thought Star.
So he raced back to Willow.

Willow threw a stick into the stream.
Splash!
"Fetch it, Star!" called Willow.

Star raced down the slope and into the stream.
Sploosh!
"Hooray!" cried Willow, "You caught it, Star."

But Star was much too far from Willow.
I'm not safe here, thought Star.
So he ran back up the slope to Willow.

"What a soggy doggy," laughed Willow.
She dried him with her scarf.
She rubbed his soggy back.

She rubbed his floppy wet ears.

Star loved it when Willow looked after him.

"Let's ramble," said Willow.
So they rambled across the wooden bridge,
into the wood and in and out of the tall, slender trees.

"Let's catch some leaves," said Willow.

Star ran and jumped.

Willow ran and jumped.

Star loved catching leaves with Willow!

Suddenly, Star heard a scuffle and a scratch.
It was a squirrel!
Star loved squirrels.

He chased it through the crinkling leaves,
this way and that.
He chased it all the way out of the wood.

Then... Star stopped.
Where was Willow?

Star had gone much too far.
I'm not safe here, thought Star.
He wished he had stayed with Willow.

Star didn't want to go back
into the wood on his own.
But Willow was in there!
I don't like being without Willow,
thought Star.
I have to go back and find her.

Star dodged between the trees.
Then he heard a small voice, calling "Star! Star!"
It was Willow!

Star wasn't frightened any more.
He raced through the trees towards the sound.
Then he saw her...

Willow!
Star raced around Willow's feet.
"You found me! What a brave dog," laughed Willow.
"Let's go home."

They left the wood with the slender trees and the crinkling leaves.

They left the splashy stream and the scuffling squirrels.

And down below…
"Look! There's our house," said Willow.
Star saw it too.

Down,

down,

down they ran.

Down to the bottom of the grassy hill,
through the gate and into the little house.

Willow curled up in the chair by the fire.
Star snuggled at her feet.
I love being with Willow, thought Star.
I love being with Star, thought Willow.